T0142522

HOW LONG SHOULD I HIDE MY CHILDHOOD HURT?

Alice Alexander-Favors

authorHOUSE®

AuthorHouse™
1663 Liberty Drive
Bloomington, IN 47403
www.authorhouse.com
Phone: 833-262-8899

Published by AuthorHouse   08/19/2022

ISBN: 978-1-6655-6730-5 (sc)
ISBN: 978-1-6655-6746-6 (e)

Library of Congress Control Number: 2022914490

Print information available on the last page.

Any people depicted in stock imagery provided by Getty Images are models, and such images are being used for illustrative purposes only. Certain stock imagery © Getty Images.

This book is printed on acid-free paper.

Because of the dynamic nature of the Internet, any web addresses or links contained in this book may have changed since publication and may no longer be valid. The views expressed in this work are solely those of the author and do not necessarily reflect the views of the publisher, and the publisher hereby disclaims any responsibility for them.

FOREWORD

Greetings to each of you, this book is an honor for me to write to help you become whole and healthy again. I have never experienced this walk myself, but I am so thankful that I had the honor to be a great listener to each of you that shared your journey with me.

On this journey it may seem to be very hard at times, long, painful and even depressing, but be encouraged you can make it.

Some of you may be saying that you have your own way of dealing with your problems and that you will share your story when you feel that you are ready and in your own way.

This is a journey. You must be ready to acknowledge all the things that have happened to you. After all this journey is totally about each of you and your feelings.

As you share your story keep in mind that you were once whole and now you are broken. Being broken don't feel good at all. God's desire is for you to be make whole.

You must be willing to accept what he (God) has to offer you so that you can become whole once again. Keep your head up step out into the next phase of your unlived new life, it will get better.

"This is from the Author's heart to each of you"

SPECIAL NOTE

The Author would like to share that all of the names, Characters, and Incidents portrayed in this book are "Fictitious".
No Identification with actual people Living or Dead,

CONTENT

Thanks for taking this journey in "How Long
Will I Hide My Childhood Hurt?"

DEDICATION

To each of you that is ready to become whole again by releasing your pass Child or Adulthood hurt. This book is dedicated to each of you. I would like to say congrats for being able to come forth and share your hurt and pain to help others as well as yourself be in a place to heal.

My prayer for you is to be able to stand firm on being able to move forward and release all your hurt and conquer all your pain both pass and present. Thanks for making this book a study tool and a part of your Library. And I pray that you will read something inside that will continue to strengthen you as you conquer your fears releasing your pain in hurt.

Thanks to my husband Pastor Calvin, who has been by my side in completing all my books. He is my biggest encourager every step of the way.

A special thanks to you babe for taking this journey with me and believing in me alone the way.

Enjoy!!!!!

Love you

CHAPTER 1

I am ready to open up and share my hurt and pain
with each of you please do not criticize me

(Sally is the Character)

CHAPTER 1

<u>Who can I trust when all else fail?</u>

Sally grew up incredibly early in life knowing that something in her house was different. She lived in fear of being molested on a regular basis by someone visiting the home. They all had something in common and that was to tell her she was not to share it with anyone what was happening to her in the home.

However, she feared being around people. She often had thoughts of telling someone what was happening at home, but she was afraid.

So even at school she would not talk to anyone about what was going on in her life, or at her home. She saw how happy others were, but she was always sad. In school one day after watching another little girl standing alone. Sally walked over to her and asked her what was her name? The girl said my name is Rosemary, and as the day went by, they became friends.

Sally knew when she saw Rosemary standing alone and not playing with the other children what was happening to her as well. Sally asked Rosemary did anyone tell her not to talk to other children. Rosemary responded yes Sally how did you know? Sally shared the same thing happened to me.

See back in the days you were not allowed to share with anyone concerning anything that took place in your home. Now we must keep in mind that uncle has also threatened Sally if she told anyone that he was going to hurt her and her family. Sally was never allowed to play outside with any other children not even her sisters. That included even the neighborhood children because that was the time that uncle would molest her. Even at school Sally would put going outside with the time uncle would molest her.

Miss James looked at Sally standing there not moving when it was time to go outside. She asked Sally is everything alright sweetie? Sally said yes Miss James, it is just I do not get to go outside at home. Miss James asked Sally if she would like to talk about it? Sally responded with no I am not allowed. Then one day Sally decided that she would go in and ask uncle if she could go outside with her sisters and why did he molest her and not her sisters? Knowing that was the time that he would molest her. Those two questions just made uncle terribly upset. Of course, uncle told Sally no and for her not to ever ask him that again he was upset.

Uncle went on to tell Sally that if she really wanted to know the reason why he molests her and not her not her sisters because she was ugly and no one else but him loved her and that was all she was good for. That really hurt sally, she cries even to this day when she thinks of what he said to her. She wanted to run away but she knew that it would hurt her mom because she did not know what was going on with her when she went to work. For the very first time Sally spoke out and told uncle how she really felt. She said uncle you said that I was fat and ugly and that no one would play with me the kids at school play with me all the time.

Uncle replied to Sally's comment by saying you are not at school so why are we still talking about this? You will never go outside while you are here, and you know while the end. Now go to your room and get ready for me to come in there. Sally, you know what time it is.

Sally went into her room and began to cry at this point she wants to tell someone. Her sisters came into the room and asked why she was crying? They asked did uncle do something to you but keep in mind that Sally could not tell anyone what he did to her, so she had to say no.

The younger sister Sue went into the room and told Uncle that Sally was crying. Uncle goes into her room and asks her why was she crying was she trying to get him into trouble? Then he told her to go wash her face and stop crying and that she better not say anything to anyone. Later uncle said to Sally that he often feared that she would tell on him soon. So, he began to threaten her every time that he would molest her.

Uncle did not work so mom allowed him to stay at home with us while she would work not knowing what he was doing to me. This would take place several times a week even at night when mom was asleep. Now Sally is trying to figure out how can she tell her mom without getting them hurt. "This is not fair to me", Sally would often say to herself. She was tired of being molested against her will. Sally and Rosemary would talk, and Rosemary told her that she must find a time to tell unless he will continue to molest her.

Sally shared with Rosemary that she was afraid of this man because he has convinced her that he would hurt all of them and that he was the only person that would ever love her. Sally told Rosemary that the way he started molesting her was by giving their private parts names. He would call his part Candy Cane and her's, Kitty Cat. But she was never to use those names with anyone else only with him. Rosemary said yes that is the way it normally starts. Sally would cry herself to sleep many nights after he left her room.

Each person deals with being molested differently. There are some that still cry as adults. Some that has been able to get it together a little better than others. There are some that do not know how to love so they make any relationship noticeably short and bitter. They do not make particularly good partners, having the trauma of being molested as a child.

It can cause them to totally be withdrawn from everyone. There are some people, after they have been molested, never leave their home again for years. They began to eat until they are over six hundred plus pounds. So due to that this has caused so many to still be afraid to share their story. They turn to food and have told themselves that eating fills that empty space inside their life. Now they are too big to come out of their house and too embarrassed to allow any one to come inside.

There are some that have not been outside in many years due to their fears, others become depressed and just give up on life all together shutting everyone out of their lives. There have been cases of some that could not handle what life had to offer them after being molested, and they committed suicide. It is especially important to seek help go to a psychologist and share your story. Psychologist will help you if you are honest, and willing to open up to them. There is help for you, but you have got to want it. There are emotions, like these that can be overwhelming that you are facing please talk to someone or write it down just get it out.

No one will ever know if you do not say anything to anyone about your pain and hurt. Some people appear to be of distressed but can cover it up well when they are faced with sharing with others what have happened to them doing the time they were molested or abused. Have you ever had a situation where you had things going on and you did not share it with anyone fear what they would think of you, knowing all the time holding it in really hurts you so badly? You are wondering what to do to ease the pain? A person that has been abused have some of the same features as a person that is has or is being molested.

If you are still hurting share, what have you done for help and how are you healing?

Emotions that you are facing can be over whelming. Please talk to someone, or write it down just get it out.

CHAPTER 2

Let the Healing Begin within
Who do I tell that I have been Molested?

CHAPTER 2

I often hear people say get over it to other people with problems not as big as sexual molestation. But it is not that easy. So, sally was always afraid to say anything to anyone thinking that they would blame her. Even as an adult Sally still feared going to therapy because of the questions she was thinking that would fail as well. She thought" what if I go to a counseling, I tell them all my concerns and it doesn't help, then what? Now the pain of hurting starts all over again.

Sally asked the question is it me? Uncle was in denial of doing anything wrong to me. Uncle said that he would say that it was my fault. And he did not do anything to me if anyone asked him. So, who would they believe me (Sally) or this guy called uncle? Some children take the fear from their childhood into their adulthood. Did you know there are some married and still live-in fear daily?

Children that have been molested are not sure how to share what they are feeling, so they began to act out in several ways because of being molested. There is that point in the children's life. No matter what you do or how loving you are, it will pull that trigger from time to time and will act out. All because they have no trust in anyone. Now that this has happened to them, they do not trust anyone.

Explain your story if you have been molested or know someone that is coping with being molested.

Does anyone know your story?

Why or why not?

CHAPTER 3

Today I am sharing all my feelings. So.
I am releasing it all to you.

CHAPTER 3

Here is one thing that I would like to share with you is that the longer a person keeps the hurt and pain inside, is the longer it takes for you to heal from the pain and hurt of being abused or molested. There are three ways you can move that is either you move forward, backwards or allow your pass to stop you in your tracks. Yes, it hurt., but it is important to find a time to release talk to someone or just write it down, but you must release it so you can begin to heal. In the lives of children, it is much harder for them to filter out what really happened to them. Or is that a normal part of life? For them. Why did it happen to them?

Children become a big puzzle when things that of the not the normal happens to them. It becomes overwhelming to them causing a new set of problems for them.

They are more· likely to carry those feelings and thoughts into their adulthood and become mean and bitter towards others, including their spouse. They seldom stay in long-term relationship because of trust issues. Please remember that trust plays an excessively big part in their lives. Be careful how you handle them. Children cannot mentally filter memories as adults do. They cannot verbally or mentally tell you what they are really feeling or what caused it.

They can tell you who did it to them but of course, not why? Please do not question them too much because they will shut down. There are adults even today that are struggling with their feelings due to being abused or molested that do not like to talk about it. In the life of children there are signs you will notice of course; all other signs are not of being molested or being abused.

Some adults can tell certain parts of what happened to them that do not hurt as bad as others. There are some that are so deep they do not like to talk about it, and will shut down. Try not to force them to talk. Just know they will talk when they are ready. Some as adults still feel very guilty when they must open up to talk with others about being molested.

Molesters will tell their victims it was their fault. They will also share with them that they are going to hurt the family if they share it with anyone else. This will have them confused. They still tear up today when they tell their story. Some children will act out in sexual inappropriate ways because they think it is their fault and they do not know how to filter it. There are children that have been molested or abused so long they think that it is normal part of life.

Some children will even use toys to act out with or other children and some will use objects. Please do not pressure them to talk about what just happened. Most likely they will get along by themselves when no one is watching and act out inappropriately. They will shut down when they feel pressure to talk about what they did. Do not make them feel as if they did something wrong by questioning them.

CHAPTER 3

Simple things to look for

Here are somethings that you can look for in both children and adults.

1. They will become distant from others.
2. Nightmares have been known to take place during the time they are sleeping after they have been arrested or abused.
3. They will also become withdrawn from others.
4. Both children and adults will get to a place where they do not want to be around others.
5. Depending on the age, wetting the bed or in their clothes both day and night can be a sign of either molested, or abuse.
   (a). Please know that these signs are not easy to detect while there are others, that are.
   (b). Always talk to the child (Adults are not as easy to talk too as children are).
   (c). Please watch for this one molester just want to hang with children vs adults. Watch your child closely at the park. Molesters love to visit parks.

CHAPTER 3

Am I the blame for what happened to me?

As Sally grew, she tried to put together the hurtful pain off her childhood and being molested. Sally said that she would cry herself to sleep some nights. She would try to figure out what happened to her in the beginning to cause the pain. Then of course, the (woo is me set in).

Now, sally is wondering what was wrong with her? Nighttime was always hard for her. Her molester would always molester her at night. Her mom would sleep hard at night. And the so-called uncle would molester her then.

The so-called uncle would always put his hand over her mouth when he walks into her room. Sally asked mom could she share the room with her sister because it was an excessively big room. But before the mom could answer the so-called uncle had responded quickly with a no Sally, you are the oldest. You need your own room. Which was far from the truth. He knew what he did to Sally at night. Sally's mom finally put this so-called uncle out. Sally is so happy now she can be with her sisters inside and outside.

Mom we can talk now, and I can share with you all that happened to me and when. Mom replied to Sally sure baby any time.

CHAPTER 4

Sally is allowing the truth to come forth

CHAPTER 4

<u>Oh no not you Dad</u>

Now sally is shocked that her dad has moved back into the house with them. Guess what? It was not long before Dad said Sally, why are you looking at me like you want me? She said no dad please, I am sorry I do not want you. Why would you say that dad want you like how? How am I looking at you? I was very young; I didn't know what he meant by saying that I wanted him. What's Sally's dad did not know was that her so called Uncle had already been molesting her. This was not new to Sally she was used to being molested and she did not like it.

There are two men in Sally's life one call himself her uncle and the other one call himself dad they both molested her at a young age. Sally finally thought why couldn't I tell my mom? But she was afraid of the family getting hurt because of her. They both told her that they would hurt her and the family. Sally is really believed that they will try to hurt the family because they both said the same thing. That they would hurt the family if she told anyone. Now she is afraid.

All of this started with Sally being molested at a noticeably young age. The only thing about the uncle is that he would give mom drinks to cause her to relax and go to bed early. Once mom goes to sleep, she would sleep until it was time for her to go to work early the next morning. See Dad came back into the family differently. He started out reading stories to my sisters and me. Even, though we are big he said we are never too big for a story. He was trying too hard to win us over. He told my sisters that they were first to get a story because they shared a room together and that I was always the last to get my story. As he came into Sally's room, he looked around and see I like this room. Then he sits down on her bed and began to rub on Sally's legs telling her to just relax as his hand would move up her leg on up to her thigh.

Explain what she could have done.

CHAPTER 4

When should I say something about my pain?

Sally really wanted to tell her mom that she was tired of being molested by the men in her life, but she loves her mom, and she did not want to hurt her and then the men hurt her to. Keep in mind these are the men that say they loved my mom so why do they keep molesting me Sally said?

But every time that she would think of telling her mom her mind would go back to the thought that both men told her the same thing and that is they would hurt the family if she said that they were molesting her. Sally has been molested since at the age of five years old. It started with them touching her and making her touch them. This went on for years.

As Sally grew and some years passed, she wanted to tell her mom that her private area was hurting, but it would lead to what happened or who did it. Did anyone touch you? She could not really explain what was happening to her body without telling her who did it to me, so she just kept quiet. Mom said it might be the soap. So, to see if that would help mom change the soap several times, but that did not help. So, after a few days went past mom asked Sally how was she feeling? At this point Mom have taken a few days off from work to take care of Sally just to find out that the problem was not the soap.

At this point, Sally has two things going on in her life, she was scared and hurting. Her birthday is coming up and she will be fourteen. She is ready to live a normal life that do not include being abused or molested. Sally wanted her birthday to be a good day to remember, so she decided to tell her mom everything that had been going on with her from the age five to fourteen years of age.

Mom is now telling Sally to remember that she is special and that she can tell her anything and that no one will ever hurt her again. All of this took place after she took Sally to the doctor and got the report of her being molested from the doctor. Sally was happy and scared. Happy that it would all be over and scared that her dad and Uncle were going to hurt the family, and she began to cry. Her mom reached out to give her a hug and asked why was she crying?

Sally asked to her mom did she remember when she told them at an incredibly young age not to allow anyone to touch their private area. Mama says yes then Sally she said, Mom uncle and Dad had sex with me when you were at work also at night when you were asleep. They told me if I told you that they will hurt me and the family. I was afraid to say anything. Mom got into defense mode asking Sally a great deal of questions. Of course, at this point, Sally, must tell the truth about everything.

Sally said "Mom, it has been happening for a long time. He hurt me so many times I could not tell you, I was scared." Sally said, "Mom the man that said he was my dad came back into our lives after being gone for years". He was doing the same thing that this man called Uncle was doing saying the same thing that he would hurt us too if I told you.

Mom, this is the time when it would happen to me when they would run bath water for you and read stories to us. He would always save me for last you would be sleep by then. He would put his hand over my mouth an abuse and molest me. When we arrived at the doctor the nurse called me back into the room to asked me to take off my clothes, and I started to cry because this is what both of them would tell me to do.

I was told to get up on the table and the doctor came in and began to check me. He looked at my mom and said mom did you know this was happening to her? Mom eyes began to fill with water, and she said no not until this week. Where are these guys, I must report them to the police today Sally yelled out Nooo! please do not let them hurt all of us. The Doctor asked Sally how long did this go on? Sally replied ever since I was five years old. Mom is still in shock crying as well. The Doctor asked mom what did she do? The doctor asked my mom if she plan to press charges on both men? The doctor shared with Sally's Mom I must call the police and make a report. Sally's mind is at ease, but she cannot help but think what will happen when they get out of jail.

CHAPTER 5

I am (Sally) Sharing even though it Hurt!!!

CHAPTER 5

<u>Should I tell even if it is my dad or my family?</u>

Sally is now opened to talk and has a lot of questions for her mom. Mom Sally said is it okay to ask you now? What should I do if it is a member of our family for real that try to have sex with me what should I do? Sally no matter who it is let me know right away said her mother.

Mom, I do not blame you said sally because I could not tell you about what was happening to me at the time. Mom, I know that you love me and would not have let anything happen to any of your children. Mom said my girls do not have to worry about this anymore. They both are going to jail the dad and the uncle. We are moving getting a fresh start in life. Please forgive me. Sally said I do mom. That bought a big smile on Sally's face. She had not smiled in a long time. To see how much her mom really cared for her and her sisters. Mom, said your dad, uncle, my friends, teachers, preachers, cousins I mean, no one is to touch any of you in no way, please tell me.

Sally is pleased now that the uncle and dad are both locked up in jail for what they did to her. Sally asks her mother what will happen when they get out of jail? Would they be allowed to come around them to visit her again, Sally is happy to finally live her life as a young girl, so she thought that the thought would go away after they went to jail. But the thought is stronger now than before, thinking of what they said that they were going to hurt the family.

Do you think Sally was brave for standing up telling her story?

What would you have done if that were you? Are you a child?

How would you have handled it differently?

CHAPTER 5

Will anyone believe me concerning my hurtful childhood? Both guys said they would blame me instead of me blaming them. They made we think that no one would believe me because I was only a kid.

Write a short respond of what you think

Write your respond of Sally's painful childhood journey thus far.

Share your story. If you to have been hurt by either being abused or molested.

CHAPTER 5

Even though I got some of my story out there is more. Mom said that since dad and uncle are locked up that I can feel free to release it more and more as I comfortable doing so, but there is no need to rush. There was no one that knew Sally was a victim of abuse or being molested in their neighborhood. So, guess what? There are thousands of people just like Sally and no one knows their story. For Sally, it was a long journey as a child. It is almost like Sally can see other people pain. People cannot look at them and tell what is going on in their life. Things would be so much better for people if they could. My hope is that no one will have to go through what I (Sally) went through in my fourteen years of life. Now, at the age of fifteen, Sally decided to share more of her story to young children. She now has friends at school that she can open up and talk to about what to do, if they are abused or molested.

Share your story Early

One day during lunch I (Sally) shared my story with a couple of friends at school. One girl went home and told her mother about Sally's story and her mother told her that she had a story to share with her concerning her childhood hurt. She said the same thing had happened to her she too was molested as a child, and she began to cry? Sally has been crippled again, this time by her mom for telling her story to too many people on the outside of the house.

CHAPTER 6

What are your concerns of Sally and
how she handled things?

CHAPTER 6

<u>Sally is still struggling with the pain as an Adult</u>

Sally had a very painful journey as we have read. As we know of Sally's story, she started being molested at the age of five years old. This went on until she was fourteen years old. She is now an adult. But the pain is still so real to her. Her childhood Is still a problem for her. Sally did not have a normal childhood. The memories of what her childhood was like constantly flash before her eyes on a regular basis.

She is looking forward to the day that she can put all of this behind her and not remember it again. Sally said if she could say one thing to help others today it would be if this have ever happened or is happening to you do not hold it in get help as soon as it happens to you and tell someone.

As Sally was thinking back over her childhood. She said this is not the way that my childhood was supposed to be. Please do not allow anyone to take your childhood from you and say anything? That is not fair. The little girl that is inside of Sally never got a chance to live out her childhood life. It is causing her today not to really know how to love as an adult in a long-term relationship and be able to trust anyone.

The greatest news is after some years Sally went to get counseling as an adult. It really seems to help her this time. After Sally visited with the psychiatrist for a while she got married. She never had any children, not yet.

Sally stated that she is not sure if children would be in her future. She said she's just learning how to deal with her emotions and her new husband. Her husband would hold her in his arms trying to comfort her. What Sally did not know is that her husband has a pass he was molested, also. He finally shared it with her. The first thought was wow, who did it to you? Now they are talking about their lives. His father molested him, and he never told anyone his mother was no longer around.

CHAPTER 6

<u>Was he really my dad the thought still flashes in my mind?</u>

At first, I knew them as friends of the family. Then as time went by, I was told to call one uncle and a short time later I was told that this one was my dad. But to me they both had two things in common and that was to molest me and tell me not to tell anyone. My so-called Dad was always. Angry. With my sisters, then I. We were afraid of him, but we could not say anything to anyone. Now, as Sally looked back at her journey, she said, sharing what happened to her head at Vantage Anna disadvantage. The disadvantage was not all the family members are mad at her for coming forth with their story concerning her dad.

The advantage is both are in jail with possibility of not getting out anytime soon. Sally is so happy that she cannot live her life normally. Without worrying about the two men and looking over her shoulders daily. But Sally says, there· is the question that still comes to mind. What if the family of those guys try to hurt me and her family?

The family of the two guys are trying to make me feel guilty. My mom said Sally your dad's family said by him going to jail he now has lost everything he ever had even the rights to visit you all. Sally said," does anyone seem to care about what he did to me?" They took my whole childhood from me. Now sally is thinking how lucky she was that she did not get pregnant from either one of them at a young age.

Sally sisters are now suspicious about what happened to Sally. They heard the rumors at school from Sally's friends as to what happened to her. They are wondering will this happen to them with Mom's next friend. Well Mom is trying to assure them that she is not bringing another guy around her girls. The next oldest girl has stopped eating afraid to gain weight.

Thinking that this will happen to her. You must know that Sally was a little on the heavy side, not fat.

The sisters put Sally's weight gain as a part of Sally's problem, Could they be putting the blame on Sally? It kind of sounds like it. But it was not her fought.

CHAPTER 6

<u>Here are a few questions from Sally's sisters</u>

Sally's sisters are now asking questions like "why did this happen to her and why didn't you tell us Sally?" Couldn't you have screamed or something? Sally replied no because he would have his hand over my mouth. Keep in mind that he always threatens to hurt all of you if I made a noise or told what he was doing to me. Trust me, I wanted to tell because I was tired of him molesting me. So, I was afraid because he had a strange look in his eyes.

Sally when did this start to happen to you? Sally said, "at the age of five". They said what? She said yes, and now I am fourteen. Nine years of pain. Sally when would this take place? She said when you all would go outside, and one sister said is that why he would not let you come outside? Sally said yes and at night when everyone was sleep.

One of the sisters said, why didn't you tell Dad? Sally said, of course Dad came in doing the same thing. Do you remember when Dad would read us stories and he would save me for last at night, but he was not really reading to me? He would do the same thing by putting his hand over my mouth so that I was not able to make a sound.

Do you remember after you all went outside the door will always be locked when you were ready to come back in? Dad said the same thing that the man that we called Uncle said that he would hurt all of you if I told anyone.

CHAPTER 7

What is your thought as a reader concerning
Sally's rough childhood Journey?

CHAPTER 7

<u>I could not say a word would they have believed me?</u>

Remember when you came inside, and I was sad you asked me if I was alright, and I did not answer you. It had just happened he had just finished molesting me and when you called him to tell him that I was crying he told me to go and wash my face and that I still better not tell anyone. It was times like that, that really frighten me. He would tell me that he would always listen in the next room when we talked.

Sally said the only person she could tell and feel safe was her Granddad (Papa) he never molested or tried to molested her. But she did not want Papa going to jail for hurting those guys, so she did not tell him either. Sally asked her sisters do they remember the day that their dad came over upset and Mom had to call the police on him? I bad told mom on him, and he was upset. Now all the sisters are afraid and wondering if someone is going to hurt them. Sally has no remorse for what she did as far as telling on both because Sally knows what it feels like for someone that has or still is being molested and they have been threatened. If they told what would happen to them.

When Sally founded out that her mother was molested at an early age, it really hurt her because mom was so hard on her as if she did not believe her at first. Sally said that her mom finally shared her story that her mom's dad molested her, and she could not tell anyone either that's why she felt that way toward Sally.

Once again, another person said he was a cousin and after a while of them being together he tried to molest her, and she told time it happened. Sally is wondering why they all bothered her. She said, now that I have had enough dad, uncle and Cousin try but I stopped him before it started. Sally has a friend at school that is going through the same thing, so I told her to tell and do it now because the longer you hold it in, the more he will do it to you.

Sarah, Sally's new friend was really shocked that Sally went through the same thing. Sarah asked Sally how did she overcome? Sally said I finally told my mom and that her mom too action against, both men. She called the police and stated what had taken place. She had to take Sally to the doctor. Sally told her that both are now in jail.

What should you do if it is **one of the following people that molest you?**

(a). The Preacher, Teacher, Dad, Uncle, Sister, Brother, or Mom no one can touch you not even any Stepparents or Siblings.

You should still tell someone.

Now that you know, the story of Sally and why she did not speak out. It was simply because she was afraid. We must remember Sally feared for her and the family as well that they would get hurt if she spoke out. Normally family do not molest family. After all of this took place, we moved regularly. Not sure if this had anything to do with the guys being released from jail. Sally knew that they were in jail because she told on them. Mom told her girls they are moving. Sally asked was it because she told on them or were, they out of jail? So, mom tried to calm Sally down by saying it's to keep you all safe when they get out. They won't know where we live. Which made Sally feel a lot better.

CHAPTER 7

Now My Teacher

Now my teacher is giving me that look that my dad gave me before he started molesting me. Today my teacher said Sally, I would like to speak with you after class when the bell ring. Sally walked up to Mr. Joe's desk, and she said yes, Mr. Joe, what is it? He said, Sally I read your School file Sally replies and what does that mean? He said that I would like for you to meet with me sometimes and it is our secret. She said no that is not right. He said you are struggling in my class do you want to fail a pass? She said, I will pass your class, but I cannot meet with you. Sally went home and told her mom what had taken place between her and Mr. Joe. So, mom said I am going to put a stop to that now. The next day Mom went out to the school and asked for a meeting with the principal and Mr. Joe. Mom told the principal what Mr. Joe told Sally. They told Sally to go to class, while the three of them talked. They moved Sally out of Mr. Joe's class, and Mr. Joe was fired at that school. Just so you know that caused Sally to withdraw again from anyone at school. She did not want to go to school again. Sally's school story.

I was truly shocked by this one

Speaking of being shocked this one was a true shocker. I bad never met a preacher and did not know how to talk to a preacher, Sarah said. My Pastor is a real cool and extremely easy to talk to man. Sally, I would like for you to go to Church with me on Sunday. But I still was afraid to talk to anyone. I asked her if she would go in with me the first time, she said yes it was ok then the second time the preacher wanted to schedule another appointment without Sarah, but I did not feel comfortable doing that, so I said no. The first appointment was an hour long. He was a good listener, long talker. So, I do not think I will go back. The preacher started to talk about the Bible while I was waiting for my mom. He invited the family to attend church services. He explained to Sally that some of the people that molest people have been on some type of drugs or alcohol before they molest people. Sally asks her mom if she would like to go to one of his services to see what it was like, and Sally Mom said yes. The Church service was nice, so we now go to church.

CHAPTER 8

How are you feeling now concerning Sally's Feelings?

CHAPTER 8

Is He Really My Uncle?

As Sally began to think of all the trouble her so called Uncle put her through, she was wondering if he was really her uncle or was that what the mom wanted them to call him. After some time went by Sally continued to attend her Therapy sections, and she became a little more relaxed with the therapy instruction. It was simply hard for Sally to wrap her head around all the things that happened to her Sally said that the mural of the story is for her to tell your story if anyone touches you in a sexual manner to tell someone.

Explain where do you turn to when you need someone to talk to?

Sally shared with her friend (Sarah) where do you go when you are not the blame? Now you want to know why you, feel useless? Sarah asked Sally has she ever heard the saying you are like a doorknob everyone gets a tum: that is how the man called uncle and my dad would do me. Sarah said she felt so nasty after all of this took place. Sally and Sarah laughed today for the first time in a long time. Sarah recommended a great Christian Counselor for Sally.

Coping with pain and anger

One day as Sally was getting ready to go to her therapy meeting she met an older lady sitting on the bench, waiting for the bus. Sally walked up to the bus stop with her head down the old lady said young lady why do you have your head down? Sally did not say anything because she did not know that she was talking to her. After a few minutes passed by the lady repeated the question. Young lady, why do you walk with your head down? She said that you are a beautiful young girl and God will protect you if you ask him. Baby have you ever prayed? Sally said no what should I pray for Ma'am?

Sally said, excuse me, ma'am. But did you say that I am beautiful? My uncle said that I was ugly and that no one would want me, and all of that has hurt me mentally. Here are some things that the old lady told Sally to do every day and it would help her to feel better. As the old lady, turned around and walk back towards Sally she said young girl do not ever let anyone tell you that you are ugly. You are valuable.

CHAPTER 8

<u>Things to do to make you feel better each day.</u>

    a.   Tell yourself that you are beautiful and brave every day.

    b.   You are strong

    c.   You are beautiful.

    d.   No matter what you see you are to feel beautiful.

<u>The Old Lady gave Sally steps to recover!!!!!!</u>

1. **<u>First step</u>**: pray daily thanking God for his protection. Sally said will God hear me I have never prayed before. The old lady told Sally try him and see he will never feel.

2. **<u>Second step</u>**: The old lady told Sally all that she must do is believe what you pray.

3. You must ask God to remove all your hurt, anger, and pain. To help you to be able to forgive the person or persons that hurt you.

4. Ask God to make you whole again, Wipe away all the tears from your eyes and replace it with joyful tears·.

5. Tell God everything and be honest because he knows all

6. Most of all forgive all that have wronged you.

7. No more crying at night over the same thing.

8. Stop! Trying to relive it. You can't blame everyone all the time for what other done to you.

CHAPTER 9

What Can you add to the list?

CHAPTER 9

When Sally did a review of what happened

Sally now sees when she began to put on weight. Her mind went back to what her uncle would say about her being fat. Sally is now up to almost six hundred pounds, and she cries every day, because she has now proven the so call man uncle as being right. So now she is going to weight therapy, to get control of her weight. Sally is learning a lot now that her counseling has really kicked in with the help of therapy. She is starting weight control classes tomorrow.

Sally said that there was no limit on her eating she would eat without even getting full. So, with that being said she would continue to eat to feel good. Sally said children were not in their future. Due to the fact Sally said that she knows that she would be overprotective over a child. She feels that her mom let her down by working so often leaving them there with a man that her and her sibling did not know. Her mom was a single mom Sally is not able to go outside now because of her weight. She is now eating different.

Paying a child not to tell while you are molesting them are never a good thing. Here are a few of the signs that a molester would do to his victims.

1. They will bribe them into not talking about what happened to them.
2. They will put fear into them. Money has been offered to some in many cases.
3. They will threaten to hurt her and the family.
4. They tell their victims that they would put the blame on them, and no one will believe that them.
5. Some have even offered their victims clothes. shoes and other items.

Sally said that uncle started out with money to keep her quiet, and her sisters would always ask where did she get the money from? She would never answer them. They said "we do our work why don't we get money?" Can you share a story of someone hurting you?

CHAPTER 9

By sharing your story how do you feel?

Why didn't you tell anyone what this person did to you?

If you told, who would you tell first?

When you see the person that molested you now, how does it make you feel?

When the Molesting took place did you live in fear? Are you fearful now?

Would you share it now verses then?

CHAPTER 10

Have depression ever crippled you in anyway?

CHAPTER 10

As you are writing, remember that this is your book or note pad, so you can write in it and only you will see it.

CHAPTER 10

What would you tell others that have been
molested and have not told anyone?

<u>Give your thought</u>

CHAPTER 10

How long shall you wait before sharing this with anyone even if they are afraid?

What would be the first advice to give anyone?

CHAPTER 10

Keep in mind that no one should touch any part of your body without your permission. No means No

There is no such thing as a good touch. If you did not want them to touch you then it's okay to tell them not to touch you and they must respect your wishes.

CHAPTER 11

Knowing good and bad touches

<u>No means no</u>

CHAPTER 11

Express your thought on how you feel now verses how you felt before you spoke out.

What could you have done differently?

CHAPTER 11

How do you really see a person that wants to be close to you after you have been molested? What will you tell them and how should you handle it?

CHAPTER 11

<u>Questions a person may have</u>

Here is a question that people always ask, are there special look that a child molester have? What is it that I should be mindful of when looking for a person that abuse or molest children or even adults? Where do they usually hang out at?

Are they in certain places? Do they talk a certain way or are they aggressive? Should I be afraid of a person like that? How do they normally approach a person?

CHAPTER 11

How many times will a molester or a person that abuses others attack? How long do they watch before they attack? If a child molester is not stopped how long will their behavior go on?

Will they really hurt the victim or their family, or is it just a threat to keep them quiet? Explain what you think

CHAPTER 12

Please keep your love one safe

<u>How can I do that?</u>

CHAPTER 12

Is there a certain gender a molester attack or will they attack anyone? What usually brings on the attack? Is it a certain way they are dressed or is it a look that they think want to say anything? Is it a known trigger that a molester have? Do they look for a certain type of person to molest? Does this mean that they have been molested as well? How common is it that the abuser is abused?

Explain what your point of view of a person that molest or abuse others

CHAPTER 12

Is there a certain pattern they look for before they molest someone?

If there is a certain look or a pattern that a molester, follow that has not been determined yet. One thing for sure, following Sally's statement they all say the same thing" if you tell they will hurt you and your family. "So, they appeared to threaten their victims before or while they are molesting or abusing them. According to Sally, they start out by introducing their body parts by giving them names so no one else would know who or what they are talking about. So, there is nothing that you can prepare yourself for.

CHAPTER 13

What should I expect when I grow up?
Do I have to look forward to this?

CHAPTER 13

Is there a chance that any one of the victims that has been molested will grow up to be a molester? Tell what you think concerning Sally's journey so far express yourself.

CHAPTER 13

How should I feel about someone who has never been in trouble before or bad not got gotten caught and now he is a molester or an abuser? Why does it seem that a person that has been molested appears to be controlling?

Give your thought.

CHAPTER 13

Most molesters attack at different times of the day and at night. So, you can never predict rather they will attack their victims doing the day or at night or both. So, if you had to share with someone about a person that molests other people, what would you say to them? Who should you tell 1st and why?

CHAPTER 14

What should you be looking for when you
are looking for signs of a molester?

CHAPTER 14

In a child there are a few signs of being molested. They become withdrawn from everyone and will shut down quickly. They will become distance from other people and children. Keep in mind that a child does not know how to express themselves like adults do. Children will begin to think something is wrong with them, and that they did something wrong or as we may say it; they are in trouble and no child likes to be in trouble.

As we know, parents often blame themselves versus getting help for their child. They do not want anyone to know what is going on in their life nor the life of the family. So, they keep all the hurt and pain on the inside without sharing it with anyone; until they just cannot handle the pain any longer.

Let us make it clear, you will need a support team when dealing with your child after being molested. There are resources that can help you to be able to help your child and keep them safe. In a child getting support or help it make a difference. They do not only help you with keeping your child safe but help you to understand the development of your child, and how to talk to them. If the child shuts down, please do not continue to question them. They will talk when they are ready.

CHAPTER 14

<u>At what age do you think a child should stop sitting on a man's lap?</u>

Sally said our grandma told us that we were big girls now and not to sit on our Papa's lap. The dad, uncle, stepparents, cousins, all should know when it's not safe to have any child sitting on their lap.

Some people say that they did not see or know that it was a problem for a girl to sit on a male's lap. Some say that their kids still at the age of sixteen and seventeen are still sitting on their dad's lap.

Some men will unconsciously get an erection when someone sits on their lap so you really should keep in mind you know when a person is on your lap that you cannot handle it.

When do you share with a child about a molester or being touched in certain areas? How soon or what age? It really depends on the age of the child. You will know when your child is really.

CHAPTER 14

How do I expose an unknown molester?

Here is some good information concerning the molester. In some cases, they have never exhibited any of this observable behavior. If you did not know of the behavior, you would not be able to tell that the person was a molester. Now anyone of any gender can be a molester. In most cases, there are more males than females that are unknown molesters.

Sally shared with us in the beginning of a story that molesters would always often start out with gifts and toys. Please watch your child at the park or someone asking about a loss. Some people asking of a lost animal is almost every molester's clue. That is one of the oldest tricks in the book. If you feel that there is a problem, contact your local toll-free hotline with any questions needed to get information on how to get the support team to help deal with a problem in crisis.

CHAPTER 15

Looking at a person you cannot tell that
they have been abused or molested

CHAPTER 15

Here are a few questions that needs answers

Will a person that has been abused or molested abuse or molest others?

Share your opinion

Yes _____   If so, why?

No _____   If so, why not?

After not being sure of what to look for in a person how can you tell the difference in a person that is and one that is not? What if the person just sexually curious verses being a molester? How can you tell?

How will you handle it when you find out the difference?

CHAPTER 15

Disabilities

Vs

Non- Disabilities

Who do you think have more of a chance of being molested or becoming a molester? The person that is disabled or the person without the disability?

CHAPTER 15

How do you think a disabled child would handle being molested or abused?

When a disabled child has become a target of a molester how should you handle the child? You must handle the situation as a normal case and get help to handle the child. The Police should always be involved in any case. A child that has been molested for a while will soon become very bitter and angry? They will lash out on anyone for the least little thing and then feel sorry after. They do not feel that therapy will help as a matter of fact they often refuse any kind of help from anyone until it is too late. Then they began to cry and eat shutting everyone out of their lives. They do not want to talk about it.

If it comes to them facing the person, they do not feel that they can do it. We must keep in mind the disabled are more at risk, especial the ones that cannot talk or do anything for themselves. There is a special target for an Autistic person. They maybe a target

The question was asked do people with disabilities normally molest other people? It has been said that people with disabilities are sexually curious more than being a molester. It has been said that their sex drive is extremely high.

CHAPTER 15

If you should see a child that is touching other children in a sexual way, how would you handle that without frightening the child? What would you do at first? Would you share it with the parent or parents?

Would think that someone has being touching the child? Some children are just curious and will act out in as sexual way.

Is this where you will share your story of how you felt because you have been in this place, or will you continue to hold on to it?

If yes, what happened. _____

Why _____ ?

If no, then why not _____ ?

CHAPTER 15

Can or will a person with a high sex drive become a molester? Give your opinion on what you think. Remember unless you share your book with someone no one will see what you are sharing.

Yes_____

Or

No_____

Why or why not?

CHAPTER 15

What do you do if there is a home with two parents and one does not believe that their child is being molester, and the other parent does? How do you handle that?

What advice can you share with the parent that does not believe? What if it is that parent that is molesting the child?

What would you do?

CHAPTER 16

Dealing with your thoughts of being molested

CHAPTER 16

Think back over your childhood did you ever touch another child while growing up being curious? Did the thought appear to your mind, but you did not follow through with it?

What caused you not to follow through with it?

CHAPTER 16

A person that is a child molester tends to rationalize their sexual needs and their behavior. Every sexual touch is not a touch of a molester.

CHAPTER 16

Worksheet

For this chapter share what you have gotten thus far out of the book. Will you be able to help anyone with the information you have?

CHAPTER 17

Sharing with your childhood feeling.

CHAPTER 17

What does this book mean to you? Would you share your feelings with others concerning this book?

CHAPTER 17

What is there for me to know about being touched?

CHAPTER 18

Here is a great concern that is extremely helpful to you. Not every person that molest the same sex is a homosexual. Yes, they use the same techniques to lure children, but they are not considered a homosexual. They know that children are more at risk from a molester or abuser.

So, you should always watch your child *I* children ask them questions without coaching them about different touches. This is a way to prevent child sexual abuse. One thing is we need to pay attention to certain behaviors please. Follow your feelings, keep that watchful eye on your child *I* children. But we should always act at the first sign of any behavior that is not normal. It is best to keep in mind how important it is to keep our children safe. If you are not sure how to handle your concern with what has taken place, with the child or children here is a resource **1-800 Child Abuse Hotline.** This does not make you a bad parent.

Some people that were molested as a child take it into their adult life, then you have others that may or may not understand what they did to another child was harmful. They will tell you that they saw mom and dad doing that to each other and they called it wrestling so the child thinks that it's OK what they are doing. You should address the behavior without pulling the child down. Calmly address the issue. Always allow the child to share with you, their feelings without questioning, them. If you feel angry the child will shout shut down. Seek help for you and your child at once especially. If they continue the behavior.

CHAPTER 18

Does anyone know your childhood story? Do you ever talk about it? How regular do you think of it?

CHAPTER 18

What is the meaning of these two words below?

a. **Molestation:** Sexual assault or abuse of a person especially.

b. **Sexual Abuse:** it is also referred to as a molestation, is abusive sexual behavior by one person upon another. It is mainly perpetrated using force by taking advantage of another person.

CHAPTER 19

Chapter 19 is the final chapter, and it contains the Author Resources.

Thanks for reading the book.

CHAPTER 19

Author Alice Alexander-Favors has written 18 books both children, an adult. You can find the books on Amazon.com, Barnes and Noble, and certain WalMart.

1. Poems of inspiration.
2. The Power of God Through a Faithful Praying Woman.
3. Men God Expect More What is your more?
4. I Have Feelings. (Children book) English only
5. Animals on the Train. (Children Book)
6. The In-Depth of the Holy Spirit (study and workbook.)
7. The Work of a Precious Little Old Country Girl.
8. How Long Will I Cry?
9. The Gardens of Insect Coloring Book. (Coloring Book)
10. Color me happy.
11. My Favorite Coloring Book
12. Color Me True.
13. He is alive
14. Let's Do the Nursery Rhyme Shuffle (Children Book)
15. Will You fight For Your Marriage, or Will You Give Up?
16. I Have Feeling /and Spanish
17. God is Looking for Men with Integrity

CHAPTER 19

Several books are being proofread

1. How Busy Are you
2. The Struggle Was Real

Author contact information

You can follow the author on her website

https:alvfavors.wixsite.com \ Alice Alexander Favors

favors615@gmail

Facebook or Instagram

(If you have a problem logging on click
the 3 lines and it should open)

Thanks for your support you can contact
me through Messenger as well

Alice Alexander Favors is an Author, Poet, Writer, Motivational Speaker. She also speaks to small groups and certain large groups. She is a woman of God and is highly active in her Faith. She is married to Pastor Calvin Favors for 37 years. Alice is the mother of four sons two of which was adopted, she is the Meme of six grands and one great grandson.

She encourages others not to never give up on their dreams and do not try to live your live to please others. Alice is a graduate of Madison High School in Madison Florida and further her education at St. Petersburg College there she received her A.A. and A.S. Degree in Early Childhood Education. Alice has some Theological experience at Life Christian University.

Alice is a person that will share with others what is helpful for them to achieve their goals ... I hope the information that is inside this book will shed some light on your story to help you be able to come forth and tell your others what happened to you and how you overcame.

I pray that this book will help you to be able to help others doing their struggles in this area of their life. They will be able to come forth with their stories of how they struggled, and it helped them to overcame.

As you can see Alice have a deep love for people. She will continue to write books, of all kinds including, Inspirational as well as Children books.

No matter what others may say you follow your mind and your dreams. Everyone thinks differently. Your dream is called your dream for a reason. When you follow you dream, you will be made complete.

THE END

Printed in the United States
by Baker & Taylor Publisher Services